KEEPER

CRYSTALS

Eve and the Rebel Fairies

For Ch is – without you there would be no
books. And because you're a rebel at heart.

First published in the UK in 2018
by New Frontier Publishing Pty Ltd
93 Harbord Street, London SW6 6PN
www.newfrontierpublishing.co.uk

ISBN: 978-1-912076-80-2 (PB)

A CIP catalogue record for this book is available from the British Library.

Designed by Celeste Hulme

Printed in China
10 9 8 7 6 5 4 3 2 1

KEEPER OF THE
CRYSTALS

Eve and the Rebel Fairies

Jess Black

Illustrated by Celeste Hulme

$\mathcal{E}$ve felt sleepy. She and Oscar had been out all day with Eve's dragon, Ingvar, enjoying the brilliant summer weather and celebrating school holidays. It was past their bedtime, but she and Oscar needed to get his bed sorted out before they could crash.

'It was nice of your gran to let me stay for a few days while Mum and Dad are away,'

Oscar yawned as he helped Eve unroll the spare mattress.

'I know. It's really cool,' Eve agreed. Her gran, Sylvie, lived next door to Oscar and his family. 'If I wasn't so tired I'd suggest a midnight snack.'

Eve grabbed a sheet and tossed it to Oscar. He tucked one corner of it under the mattress but as he turned his back a large dragon snuck her snout under the sheet's edge.

'Ingvar!'

Eve laughed. 'She loves playing hide and seek.'

Oscar pulled a face and whispered to Eve, 'I hate to break it to her but it's pretty hard to hide if you're a large purple dragon.'

Ingvar snorted and the sheet billowed into the air from the force.

'I think she heard you,' Eve laughed.

'Ingvar!' Oscar said sternly. 'Now I have to start all over again.'

'She'll do it twenty times until you finally give up and play with her,' Eve said with a grin, kneeling down to retrieve the sheet that had fallen to the floor under her bed. As she grabbed hold of it, she noticed something pink against the wall.

'Oh, wow!' Eve sat up, pushing the sheet aside. She pulled her bed back from the wall and kneeled down again.

'What is it?' Oscar asked.

'It's my old fairy door,' Eve exclaimed and stood back for Oscar to see. 'I had completely forgotten all about it.'

Attached to the wall, at floor height, was a miniature pale-pink door with a shiny gold handle.

'It's teeny tiny!' Oscar said.

'Duh!' Eve nudged him. 'It's *fairy*-sized.

Haven't you ever seen a fairy door before?'

'Um, it's not really something boys are into,' Oscar admitted.

Ingvar shuffled forward to see what the fuss was about, crouching low with her head between her claws. Eve could feel the dragon's whiskers tickle her arm as Ingvar put her head closer to sniff the door.

Eve traced the door's outline with her fingers. 'I used to love this when I was little. I would lie awake at night, imagining the fairies coming in and out. They might come to take a tooth from under my pillow or even just roam around Gran's house. I'd try to stay awake long enough to see one but I always drifted off.'

Ingvar sneezed and snuffled into Eve's arm. 'Do you want to see what's inside, Ing?' Eve teased. 'We're a bit too big to fit through the door.'

'What's the box?' Oscar asked.

'It's a letterbox for fairy mail, of course!' Eve smiled as she opened the tiny lid. A tingling sensation rippled down her fingers. 'I used to write the fairies letters and that's where I would leave my teeth for the tooth fairy.'

Eve's fingers brushed against something solid inside the box and she pulled it out. As she did so she felt her cheeks flush and the tingling feeling returned, stronger this time.

'It's a fairy!' Eve looked up at Oscar, her eyes wide. 'A miniature crystal fairy.'

Eve and Oscar never knew where Eve's gift as a crystal keeper would take her next, or which mythical creature would summon her for help. They had met a golden phoenix, a unicorn and even a griffin on their adventures. Each time a crystal would appear, and it would act as a portal to transport her into another world. Like the others, this tiny crystal in the shape of a fairy left an imprint on Eve's hand that burned and prickled her skin.

Oscar immediately grasped Eve's shoulder and made sure he was in contact with Ingvar. If they were all together, Oscar and Ingvar could join Eve in whichever world she was called to.

A loud noise erupted in their ears, like the sound of something tearing. Eve felt her body grow heavy and she realised she was shaking.

'I don't feel so good,' Oscar whispered. Eve squeezed his hand. She didn't feel too good either, but she tried her best to remain calm.

Then her body began to shrink.

'We're getting smaller!' Eve cried. Her muscles ached, and her body felt as if it was being pulled this way and that. She could see herself shrinking. First she was the height of her dresser, then her desk, then all of a sudden she was only as tall as her bed. She looked at Oscar and Ingvar. They were both getting smaller and smaller too.

Eve felt dizzy and her head began to spin. All too soon she was looking up at her bed and it seemed as big as a hill. The handle on her bedroom door seemed as far away as the top of a tall building!

'I think I'm going to be sick,' Oscar groaned. Ingvar hissed. She let out little puffs of smoke which grew smaller and smaller in size.

Just as Eve thought she couldn't stand it any longer, the aching stopped. She looked down at herself. She was the same Eve but a miniature version. Even her clothes had shrunk!

'Wow.' Eve stared at her hands and her arms. 'I'm the size of a Barbie doll! This is *so* weird.'

'It's a bit freaky!' Oscar agreed, looking dazed. 'We've never been ... *shrunk* before.'

Standing against the fairy door, Ingvar

looked just like a small toy dragon. 'Ing, you're so cute!' Eve exclaimed. The dragon snorted in protest and let out a blast of fire.

'I don't think she likes being called cute!' Oscar chuckled.

'Sorry Ing – you're very tough even though you're tiny.' Eve held out her palm with her miniature fingers outstretched. 'It happened because I touched the crystal.'

Printed on her palm was the tiny outline of a fairy. This is what it meant to be a crystal keeper, for Eve and for Eve's gran Sylvie. Creatures in distress called to them through the crystals, and Eve had no choice but to respond. Oscar had been with Eve for all of their adventures, and now Ingvar, Eve's kindred animal, also joined them wherever they went. The worlds could be dangerous, and the three friends never knew what to expect.

'So, what now?' Oscar asked, looking around at the now vast bedroom. 'It could take days just to make it to the other side of the room.'

Eve glanced down at the small imprint of the fairy on her palm. She felt the magic of the crystals and concentrated on speaking to the fairy in her mind. *Are you there? Don't be afraid. We are here to help.*

Eve heard nothing back. She met Oscar's gaze and shrugged.

Just then they both heard a click and turned around. The fairy door opened and a small green face appeared. It was a girlish face with large pointy ears and a small green pointed hat on top of it. What was even more startling was that the large green eyes were staring intently at Eve.

'Hello!' exclaimed Eve. 'Did you call us here?'

The creature giggled and, just as quickly as she had appeared, she vanished again, leaving the fairy door slightly ajar.

'Odd-looking fairy,' Oscar muttered.

'That wasn't a fairy. That was a pixie,' Eve corrected him.

Oscar raised an eyebrow. 'That's one of those details that only a girl would know.'

Eve smirked but her attention was drawn to the fairy door. 'Where did she go? I can't see anything but a dark tunnel.'

Oscar held the fairy door open for Eve. 'Ladies first!'

Ingvar leaped through ahead of them, her spiky tail disappearing into the tunnel. Oscar look one last lingering look around Eve's colourful and familiar room.

'Let's get going!' Eve urged. She grabbed his hand and pulled him through the door.

Inside the tunnel, they couldn't see the pixie but they could hear her cheeky giggling somewhere in the distance. Stumbling along in the gloom, they followed the sound and held onto the damp walls. Before long the tunnel fell away to reveal a green countryside that was so picturesque it looked like a postcard.

'Fairyland,' breathed Eve. 'It's beautiful.'

She could see a bubbling stream adorned with mossy stones on either side. Delicate blossoms in shades of violet and pink grew in bunches of colour that broke up the green palette. Even Oscar was lost for words and Ingvar purred her appreciation.

A familiar green hat poked out from behind a large rock.

Oscar pointed. 'There's our little friend!' The pixie darted behind the rock again and disappeared.

'Wait!' Eve called. 'We've come to help!'

'Hey, Ingvar.' Oscar placed a hand on the dragon's shoulder and mounted her strong back. 'Let's catch this little green runaway.' He held a hand out for Eve and pulled her up to sit in front of him.

'Follow that pixie!' Eve cried.

Ingvar launched into the air and began to fly.

lying on the back of a dragon never grew old for Eve. What made it even better was that Eve and Ingvar could communicate without Eve speaking. She would concentrate her thoughts towards the dragon and Ingvar understood her. They had a very special connection.

That's it Ing, Eve said in her mind, *get down nice and low.*

It was difficult to keep up with the pixie. She was so sure-footed and quick. 'She's a happy little critter,' Oscar remarked from behind Eve. 'I just wish she'd slow down!'

Eve knew they would need to fly in front of the pixie and cut her off to have any chance of catching her. She steadily guided Ingvar lower and lower as they gained on the pixie. The little creature paused at a river crossing and Eve yelled, 'Now!'

Ingvar swooped down low and skidded bumpily to the ground. Eve threw herself off Ingvar's back and ran to the water's edge. 'Please wait!' she cried.

This time the pixie didn't run away. She blushed a deeper green and giggled again.

'What's so funny?' Eve asked.

'Thank you, Marmite,' came a light and tinkly voice from behind them. Eve swung around.

15

She was looking right at a fairy.

'Whoa. An actual real-life fairy,' whispered Oscar.

The creature looked a little like a young girl but she had the most magnificent pair of golden wings sticking out behind her shoulders. They looked like they had been spun from pure gold. Her hair was dark brown and shoulder-length, her eyes were bright blue and her ears were pointed.

Eve felt the mark on the palm of her hand tingle and grow hot. This had to be the fairy who had called them here.

'You must excuse us for the way we have brought you here. I wanted you to arrive swiftly and appear to have come on your own,' the fairy said. Her voice sounded like a flute – as if she could somehow speak words from the notes themselves.

'I am Eve and this is my friend Oscar. And

Ingvar is the dragon.'

'I am Orla, the Golden Queen of the Fairies.' The fairy took Eve's hand and her skin felt smooth and warm. Eve noticed that little particles of glittery dust filled the air as Orla moved. 'Come with me.'

Orla was barefoot but she moved swiftly through the thick grass and ferns along the side of the river. Marmite had vanished, and it was just for the four of them.

They walked in silence. At one point Oscar opened his mouth to speak but the fairy hushed him. Eve realised she would talk only when she was ready.

Finally, the thick ferns fell away to reveal a small clearing protected by moss-covered boulders and ancient twisted brambles. A gathering of some ten fairies looked up at their approach. They were male and female, all barefoot with fine spun-silk clothing and wings, although none as impressive as Orla's.

Each fairy approached and took Eve by the hand, then did the same with Oscar. Ingvar received a gentle pat from each one. Eve was completely covered in the glittery dust by the time the greetings had finished.

'Sit.' Orla lifted her graceful arm and indicated a smooth stone bench. Eve and Oscar sat while Ingvar stood guard next to Eve. Eve gave her snout a reassuring rub.

'Thank you for coming,' Orla trilled as another fairy presented Eve and Oscar with a small acorn each. Eve brought the acorn to her lips. It contained the clearest, most thirst-quenching water she had ever tasted. She felt better immediately. Oscar drained his in one gulp and looked up with a goofy grin.

'Tasty?' Orla enquired with a smile.

'Very.' Oscar wiped his dripping chin with the back of his hand.

'Why do you need our help?' Eve asked.

'We have brought you to the fairy realm. It is not a place that humans can see but it exists alongside your own human world.'

Eve nodded. This made sense to her.

'Fairies are responsible for creating the natural world you enjoy on Earth. We grow the flowers, shape the clouds, create the jungles, fertilise the fruit ... you get the idea?'

'That sounds like a lot of work,' Oscar said, impressed.

'It is,' Orla chuckled, 'but we have lots of help in the form of pixie dust. Pixie dust is the dust that allows fairies to fly. But it has other magical qualities that help us to make the plants grow.'

'So it's not just a fairy story?' Eve asked.

'You're saying that pixie dust is *real*?'

Orla laughed and a few of the other fairies giggled quietly. 'It's real, alright.' Orla opened a small cloth bag that was tied to her waist and scooped up a handful of coloured dust. She sprinkled the dust onto the grass beside them and whispered a few words.

Eve watched in awe as a tomato vine began to grow around a stake right in front of them. The small green tomatoes swelled in size until they were large and red and ripe.

'That's incredible!' Oscar gasped. Ingvar let out a snort.

'We gather all of our pixie dust from the pollen of one tree. It is the source of all of our power. This tree – we call it the Tree of Life.'

At the mention of the name of the tree Eve felt the mark on her hand grow hot and begin to throb. She knew immediately that whatever was wrong here related to this tree.

Orla's expression grew grim. 'But two fairies have begun to use up the dust for their own purposes. Our tree only produces a certain amount of dust at a time and we need it for many things. The whole world could be in danger if we cannot fly or grow food or protect the trees and creatures.'

'That sounds terrible,' Eve exclaimed.

'That's just the beginning,' Orla continued. 'They have been seriously disrupting the balance of both our world and yours. We've already had to rescue a few humans and animals, not to mention pixies and fairies. These two young fairies think they're having a bit of fun, but what they are doing is dangerous to others.'

As Orla talked Eve rubbed at her palm,

the one with the fairy mark on it. She felt tingly and flushed.

'Have you ever seen a hot-pink river?' Orla continued. She lifted her hand and scattered a handful of dust into the air. It created a sparkling wall that morphed into a screen. A very lifelike picture emerged of a river the colour of pink zinc dotted with neon-orange rocks.

'That looks really trippy,' Eve said.

'It's not naturally this colour. By doing this, the rebel fairies could poison the fish who live in it and affect animals that eat the fish.' Orla flicked her wrist and the image changed to a blueberry-coloured sunset with black-and-white patchwork clouds stretched across the sky. 'Nor is this sunset a natural one. Now some creatures will think it's night when it's still daytime and nocturnal animals will become confused.

It's already created complete havoc. These are just two examples out of many. We've had to divert floods, stop rockfalls and even remove wings from animals that were never meant to fly.'

'I see what you're saying,' Eve nodded.

'It also means all of the other fairies have to redo the work, which of course uses up more of our precious pixie dust.'

'Where are these rebel fairies?' Eve asked. 'How do we stop them?'

'I was hoping you would ask that,' Orla nodded solemnly. 'We will find them tonight at the Tree of Life, stealing our pixie dust.'

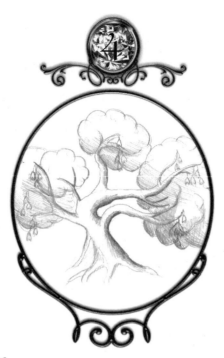

The rest of the day passed quickly. Eve, Oscar and Ingvar were made to feel at home in the fairy glen and they passed the time chatting with a few of the less shy fairies. They even forgot that they were pint-sized because everything in the fairy world was so small.

Oscar got along really well with a male fairy named Aubrey, who delighted in being shown how to play soccer using a coconut as a ball. Eve had her hair braided with colourful ribbons and tried on a fairy dress. The soft material felt light as air and clung to her body like a second skin. She didn't have wings or pointed ears, but she looked more fairy-like and would blend in more easily with the scenery. When she took off her shoes, it felt almost as if she might be able to fly.

What Eve and Oscar both enjoyed most of all were the fairy skills their new friends taught them: how to scale a tree in seconds and use their colouring to blend in with the plants and trees around them.

Ingvar took the opportunity to sleep and curled up comfortably on one of the toadstools that the fairies used as chairs. Her gentle snores caused the fairies to giggle quietly.

'Tell me more about how the fairy world works,' Eve asked Orla as they nibbled on a plateful of fresh strawberries.

'Most of the stories you were told as a child are true,' Orla began. 'We come and go, unseen, between our world and yours. We can grant wishes. We don't like goblins.'

There was something that had always troubled Eve so she took the opportunity to ask. 'What do you do with all of the human teeth you collect?'

Orla's eyes sparkled in amusement. 'We send them up to the night sky to become stars.'

Eve gasped. 'That's beautiful.'

Orla nodded. 'We try to recycle as much as possible when we create the natural world. We look at the Earth so closely from our small viewpoint. Every living thing has something to teach us and is worthy of our respect and care.'

'It must be awful for you to see what humans do to the natural world,' Eve mused sadly.

'Yes, Eve,' Orla agreed, 'and this is why the fairies Lilith and Azura have decided to take matters into their own hands. They want to play havoc with nature to get humans' attention. But they are in great danger of destroying your precious world – and ours. And that means they will destroy all of us along with it.'

When the sun went down and the moon was just visible on the skyline, Orla announced that it was time to leave. Aubrey had asked to join them and Oscar looked pleased to have some male company. As they set out in single file in the direction of the Tree of Life, a giggle revealed that Marmite had also joined their search party.

'They're certainly a puzzle, the pixies!' Orla murmured. She had noticed Eve staring at the green creature with fascination. 'We couldn't do without them. It's their dust and they're happy for us to use it as long as we keep the world in balance. We need them and they need us.'

'Can't they stop the thieves by refusing them dust from the tree?' Eve asked quietly.

'Lilith and Azura tricked a pixie into giving them permission. It cannot be undone,' replied Orla grimly.

The sky grew dark and with the moon behind a blanket of clouds it was tricky to see where they were going. Orla created a fine sprinkling of pixie dust to light their way. It was like being followed by a group of twinkling stars. Despite the trouble there might be up ahead, Eve couldn't help but be mesmerised by the fairy world and all its beauty.

'There is the tree.' Aubrey stopped and pointed.

Ahead of them on a sloping hill stood the majestic Tree of Life. It looked like an evergreen from Earth, but it had enormous silver branches that radiated a bright white glow and dainty silver blossoms hanging in bunches below. What was even more impressive was that the tree made a sound like the humming of bees. It was alive and crackling with magic.

'Shhh.' Orla put her finger to her lips. 'I can hear them.'

Eve listened but could only hear the sound of Ingvar's breathing and the tree's low hum. Then a shadowy figure appeared, walking lightly towards the tree. Ingvar let out a hiss. Eve tickled her under her bristly chin to calm her.

'That's them,' Orla said in a low voice.

There were now two figures beneath the tree, standing close to its gnarled trunk. 'That's Azura and Lilith.'

The fairies were close enough to the tree for its light to reveal their faces. Eve was surprised to see that they looked just like the other fairies she had met that day. They were beautiful young girls in coloured dresses, with braided hair and large, delicate wings. She had expected them to look somehow different.

Azura and Lilith set about picking handfuls of the silver blossoms and placing them into a large sack. As they did, Eve noticed the light from the tree dim slightly and fade, and the humming sound grew more faint. They were stripping the tree of its magic.

Eve was itching to confront the two reckless fairies but Orla had told her and the others to stay hidden and watch. As Azura and Lilith laughed and headed off in the opposite direction, Eve wanted to scream.

'What are we going to do?' Eve whispered urgently.

'As the Golden Queen I am helpless to take action against one of my own.' Orla took Eve's hand and with a dust-coated finger she traced the mark of the fairy on Eve's palm. 'This is where I leave you. Follow them, Eve. Take your friend, your dragon and Aubrey with you. The fate of both of our worlds is in your capable hands.'

Eve nodded. She had no idea how they were going to stop the thieving fairies but she knew she had to try – before they did something terrible that even fairy dust couldn't fix.

ve and her friends followed Azura and Lilith from a safe distance. The fairies were wild and thoughtless, and took great delight in using the pixie dust to make trouble wherever they went.

Azura fell about in fits of giggles after giving a surprised-looking fieldmouse a pair of wings and a tortoise spots like a leopard, and Lilith caused the water in a waterfall to flow backwards, flooding the river above.

'They're out of control!' Eve muttered under her breath.

They tailed the fairies all night and grew tired of their trickery very quickly. Aubrey was so angry that he stopped speaking. He had used up most of his pixie dust to undo their pranks and set things right again. Every trick they played shifted the balance of nature – not just in the fairy world but in the human world too.

'I've had enough of watching these two cause trouble. I'm going to speak to them,' Eve resolved. It was dawn, and the fairies were sitting down in a sheltered grove to feast on a breakfast of fresh pineapple. They looked sleepy after their night of misbehaviour.

'I'm coming with you,' Oscar declared. 'There is no way I'm letting you confront those troublemaking fairies alone.'

Eve agreed. 'Aubrey, you and Ingvar stay hidden but watch closely. We might need your help.'

Aubrey raised an eyebrow and sat nervously alongside Ingvar, who pawed at the ground in protest. She hated being left out of the action and she never liked being too far from Eve.

'Hello, fairy folk.' Eve gave the two fairies a wave as she approached. Her heart was racing. She was aware these two could use their magic on her but she needed to stand her ground.

'A human?' Lilith jumped to her feet in surprise but Azura stayed still. 'Ooh, and dressed like a fairy. How *quaint*.'

'I'm Eve and this is my friend Oscar.'

'How did you get here?' Azura's eyes turned to slits as she scowled at them.

'I am a crystal keeper. I have magical powers too. I'm here to ask you to stop abusing your powers and leave the natural world be.'

Lilith made a show of yawning: 'Blah, blah, blah. I'm so bored that I'm falling asleep right now.'

Azura looked Eve up and down and didn't seem impressed by what she saw. 'Oh? And how do you think you're going to make us stop?' she laughed. Oscar huffed and glared at her.

'I can't make you do anything but I can appeal to you,' Eve replied, calmly. 'You're causing damage in both our worlds. I'm worried that it could get out of hand and possibly hurt someone.'

Azura burst out laughing. 'You've got a nerve, human. You think you can come into my world and tell me what to do?' She waggled her finger from side to side. 'I don't think so.'

'Don't talk to Eve like that!' Oscar took a step forward.

'It speaks!' Lilith teased.

Oscar shot her a withering look but kept quiet as Eve placed a warning hand on his arm. She sensed that these fairies could be easily provoked into doing something they all might regret.

'You've had your fun. Now it's time to stop.' Eve's tone was firm. 'You have a choice. You can look at the work you do as boring or you can see the beauty of it.' Eve's eyes lit up as she spoke. 'You create life! There's nothing more perfect than the petals in a flower, the colours on a bird's feathers, the wonder of a sunset. You are artists! Our world would be desolate without you.'

As Eve spoke she realised just how true

36

this was. Even though she lived in the city she loved being out in nature and with animals. It was where she felt completely happy.

'You humans have an odd way of showing your appreciation,' Azura snapped. 'You dig up the ground to build skyscrapers, shopping centres and car parks. You leave your rubbish everywhere to pollute the soil and choke animals and sea creatures. You don't deserve our works of art.'

'You're right, Azura,' Eve admitted. 'There are people who don't care for the Earth as they should. But we're not all like that.'

'Duh!' pouted Lilith. 'Haven't you heard of a thing called global warming? The sea levels are already rising!'

'Humans need a wake-up call – I agree. And it *is* time we did something dramatic. But not like this!' Eve pleaded.

'The time for talking is over,' Azura shrugged. 'Now you humans need to be taught a lesson.'

Lilith smiled at her friend. 'Are you thinking what I'm thinking?'

Azura nodded. 'I think Miss Bossy Boots here needs a makeover – and her puppy dog sure does!'

Before Eve could move Lilith threw a pinch of pixie dust in her direction. The rainbow-coloured sparkles settled on Eve's head and shimmered down her entire body. She felt a slight tingling sensation.

'A taste of your own medicine, human!' Lilith muttered a few words in a language Eve didn't understand.

'What's happening, Eve?' Oscar asked. His voice sounded strange.

Azura snorted with laughter. She locked eyes with Lilith and the two flew away.

Eve heard the sound of a dog whining. She looked around for the source of the noise.

Oscar was a boy no longer. He was now a black poodle, complete with a bright blue ribbon around his neck. He looked up at her with wide brown eyes and panted.

'Oscar?' Eve stared in horror at the canine version of her best friend.

'Woof!' Oscar replied. Then he growled.

Eve felt very strange. She realised her body was changing too and tried desperately to call on her own powers. They had no effect.

'What's happening, Oscar?' Eve looked down at her own body and realised with alarm that instead of hands she had pincers, and instead of two legs she had six.

The fairies had turned her into a large black beetle!

It was more than a little scary to be sniffed at by a big black dog, especially when you had been shrunk to the size of a beetle. Eve quivered inside her hard black casing and her long legs twitched nervously.

'Please don't eat me, Oscar,' she begged. As Eve spoke she realised her voice had changed too. Instead of words the only sound that came out of her mouth was a soft clicking.

Oscar whined but only gave her a big sloppy lick before bounding off.

Ingvar snorted loudly and a lick of flame escaped her nostrils. *It's okay Ing,* Eve assured her dragon friend. *I won't look like this for much longer.*

Eve hoped these words were true. She did not like the feeling of scuttling along the ground on her many legs and was feeling a very strong urge to eat a fly.

Aubrey had flown back to the Tree of Life to get more pixie dust. In the meantime, Eve cowered under a large green leaf, hoping nothing would eat or squash her while Aubrey was gone.

Ingvar lay on the ground next to her. The spiky dragon snout looked even more enormous to Eve now. *And I thought a fairy*

was small! This is even worse! Eve thought. But she also realised just how different it was to be in nature when you were so close to the ground.

Finally Aubrey returned. The dark magic was quickly reversed with new dust and a few words from their fairy friend. Eve felt that queasy feeling as her body changed again and took a new form. Soon she was herself again – even if she was fairy-sized!

'I don't ever want to be a beetle again,' Eve sighed in relief. 'Although you make a very cute poodle, Oscar.'

'Ha, ha.' Oscar wasn't impressed. 'Now I know what it feels like to chase your tail.'

'I have some bad news,' said Aubrey. 'I've just heard from Orla. While we were changing you back into human form, Lilith and Azura flew into the human world, started melting a glacier, turned all sharks vegetarian … and something else about a flock of green sheep?'

'They've gone too far!' Eve exploded in exasperation. 'If the glacier melts, the sea levels will increase and flood coastal areas. People will die!'

'And the sharks? If the animal food chain is altered it will affect every sea creature,' added Oscar, shaking his head.

'No more talking! We have to find Azura and Lilith *right now* and put an end to this!' Eve sprang onto Ingvar's back and Oscar quickly followed. Aubrey didn't need help flying as he had his own stunning wings.

'In order to go back to the human world – even flying on a dragon – you need to cross the troll bridge,' Aubrey called as they soared higher and higher into the sky.

'Don't you mean *toll* bridge?' Oscar answered.

'*Troll.* And not a cute colourful one, like you've seen in movies. I'm talking about a big scary monster that likes to sleep under bridges … oh, and that eats humans.'

'I have a bad feeling about this,' Oscar muttered, clinging onto Eve as Ingvar dipped and soared through the clouds.

Eve remembered stories from when she was younger about trolls. They were always enormous and always grumpy. She wondered why.

'Can you tell us more about the troll?' she asked Aubrey as they flew.

'Trolls leave us alone, but the reason this troll was put under the bridge was to guard it in case humans entered the fairy world. I'm fairly sure he's had nothing to do for the last few thousand years.'

'And then two humans and a dragon

appear! He'll be very hungry by now, don't you think?' Oscar whispered to Eve.

'Here we are.' Aubrey flew down to the ground. 'You're on your own for this next bit. I can't interfere – it's part of fairy law.' He shrugged.

'Convenient!' Oscar clapped Aubrey on the back and smiled.

Aubrey nodded but looked uncertain.

'It's okay,' Oscar said. 'We'll see you on the other side.'

Aubrey gave the trio a thumbs up and took off in the direction of the far side of the bridge. Eve gazed after him longingly.

'Let's get this over and done with, shall we?' Oscar asked her with a wink. 'If anyone can charm a troll then it's you, Eve.'

'Why thank you!' Eve replied with more confidence than she felt.

The bridge looked very old and was

constructed of old sandstone and rock. It was also covered in a thick layer of moss. Eve, Oscar and Ingvar stepped tentatively onto the rough stone pieces and began to cross the bridge.

'I don't see a troll, do you?' Oscar whispered.

'No, but they used to hide *under* bridges,' Eve replied. 'We have to go down there.' She pointed to the area under the bridge hidden beneath a blanket of green foliage.

'I'm pretty sure that girls taste better than boys,' Oscar said mischievously.

'You're probably right,' Eve agreed, 'but nobody is being eaten today.'

When they had taken a few steps, Eve paused. She could feel the ground beneath her vibrate.

'Hello, Troll?'

There was a pause and then a terrible

rumble. Eve could hardly believe her eyes as she watched the moss and stone to the side of the bridge move and peel away to become the shape of a large creature. It had long green mossy hair that covered most of its face.

Eve gulped. The troll looked just like trolls she remembered seeing in her picture books when she was a little girl. It also smelled like rotting vegetables.

'Phooey,' Oscar muttered under his breath.

Eve shot him a look.

'Human children.' The troll's voice was deep and gravelly. The bridge shuddered and creaked as the troll spoke.

'I am Eve. I am a crystal keeper. I need to stop some fairies creating chaos in our world and yours. May we pass?'

The troll took a few lumbering steps

forward. The stench was overpowering, like putrid mud and rotten eggs. He inhaled deeply.

'You smell good.' He licked his lips as he spoke.

'Don't you come a step further!' Oscar warned.

'I haven't smelled a human for thousands of years!'

'Please don't eat me,' Eve said, keeping her voice steady. 'We need to cross the bridge to help save Earth.'

'You look like you'd go well with a little mint on the side.'

The troll reached out an earthy hand with long dirty fingernails and made a grab at Eve. Ingvar puffed herself up to her full height and let out a terrifying roar. Flames poured out of her nostrils, searing the troll's mossy fringe and revealing his face completely. He had eyes as large as saucers and a long thin nose. He was very ugly.

'I can *see!*' the troll cried in delight.

'You did need a haircut,' Eve agreed.

The troll's manner changed completely. He smiled and looked slightly less terrifying when he did so. Then he shuffled from side to side in what looked like a happy dance. 'Thank you!' he cried.

Ingvar huffed warily.

'I haven't been able to see for thousands of years. It's made me very cross not knowing who was talking to me.'

'A good haircut can do wonders,' Oscar agreed.

'You can cross my bridge.' The troll stepped aside.

Eve breathed out deeply in relief. 'Thank you.'

'*If ...*' the troll continued.

Eve looked up sharply.

'*If* you bring me back my favourite snack. After humans, it's those cheesy-flavoured chips that look like triangles.'

'Corn chips?' Oscar asked.

The troll shuddered with delight. 'That's the one! Corn chips!'

'It's a deal,' said Eve. 'Now we really have to hurry. How does this bridge work?'

'Walk across and think about where you want to be. And that's where you'll arrive.'

'Thank you, Troll!' called Eve.

'Actually, my name is Percy!'

ve reached the end of the cobbled bridge and faced a veil of sparkling pixie dust. When she reached out her fingers to touch it her hand disappeared into the shimmering wall.

'I'll go first,' Eve said as she stepped inside.

Aubrey looked very relieved to see them emerge from behind the moss-covered veil that separated the fairy world from Earth.

As beautiful as the fairy world was, Eve felt a strong sense of relief at being back on the planet she knew and loved.

'How did you get past the troll?' Aubrey asked, impressed.

'Turns out he loves food of all shapes and sizes!' Eve smiled. 'Remind me that we need to go shopping on our way back or he might decide to eat us after all. But where is the glacier?'

'Look behind you,' Aubrey said.

Eve spun around. Where the shimmering wall had been was a huge mass of ice and snow. Eve had never seen a glacier in real life and it was much bigger than she expected. They were standing on top of a tall mountain, and the jagged edges of hard-frozen snow wound their way from the top to the very bottom of the valley below. Just as Eve had feared there was a small village further down in the valley. Those houses would be swept away in a flash flood if the glacier melted.

'It's huge, isn't it?' Oscar marvelled. 'Especially as we're all still fairy-sized!'

'It takes many many years to form,' Eve agreed. 'It's beautiful.'

The glacier was breathtaking but also a little scary. Waterfalls dripped, ice cracked, and crags jutted out at all angles. Eve could even hear the faint sound of creaking as the ice moved. It was ancient and majestic.

'There they are!' Aubrey pointed.

Sure enough, Lilith and Azura were not far from them, standing on top of a pointed crest of the glacier. But they didn't look like they were having fun. Eve realised with a jolt that something was wrong.

'Quick!'

Ingvar flew them swiftly towards the

fairies until they were above the white and blue ice, which was streaked with dirt. Up close the glacier was very different. Eve realised immediately it would be treacherous to try to walk on it without the proper equipment. The ice wasn't flat like it first appeared from a distance. It was made up of steep icy steps and deep cracks that fell into a dark abyss below.

'What's happening?' Eve asked as Ingvar hovered near the two distressed fairies.

'Our wings are wet. We can't fly!' cried Lilith.

'The ice is melting,' shrieked Azura as she gripped Lilith's hand.

The faint creaking and cracking sound Eve had heard earlier was getting louder. Eve realised that the ice was beginning to thaw.

'Here,' Eve reached her hand out to Azura. 'Take my hand. I'll pull you up onto Ingvar's back.'

Azura wavered.

'How do I know I can trust you?' she gasped.

'You turn me into a beetle and you wonder if *I'm* the trustworthy one?' Eve countered.

There was a loud crack and the ice beneath the fairies began to break apart. Lilith screamed. The gap between her feet widened as the ground moved beneath her. The expanding crevasse below was sheer and deep.

'Come on!' Oscar yelled as he reached out for Lilith's hand.

Azura lurched forward and collided with Ingvar's tail. She lost her balance and fell. As she tumbled she knocked Lilith over and the two fairies fell in a tangle of hands and feet, scratching desperately for a grip on the ice as the crevasse opened alongside them.

'Azura! Lilith!' Eve called out. She sprang off the dragon's back and dived forward onto the ice, just managing to catch hold of Lilith's ankle. Azura had slipped down into the deep crack and was clinging to Lilith, and Lilith was suspended upside down in the air.

Eve's arm ached with the pain of carrying their weight. 'I can't hold them ...' she cried out, gritting her teeth and again trying to channel her crystal power.

'We can't land here!' Oscar shouted, as Ingvar hovered desperately. Out of the corner of her eye Eve could see Aubrey flying as fast as he could around the glacier, sprinkling pixie dust to try to steady the ice.

'Hold on, Eve!' Oscar shouted. But the ice shifted once more. With an explosive crack the crevasse widened, and the shudder caused Eve to lose her grip on Lilith's ankle. The two fairies fell into the dark below and were gone.

'Lilith!' Eve called into the long, deep crack in the ice. 'Can you hear me? Azura?'

There was no reply. The only sound on top of the vast mound of ice were the cracks and drips of the ancient glacier moving and shifting. Then Eve heard a voice.

'Help us!'

'I see them!' Eve realised the fairies' fall

had been broken by a ledge of ice sticking out of the crevasse. They were clinging to it.

'I'm not sure how long this ledge will hold our weight,' called Lilith.

'We'll get you out as fast as we can,' Eve called back. She turned to Aubrey, who was fluttering anxiously beside her. 'Aubrey, can you use the pixie dust to help the girls fly back up?'

'I can't spare any more dust right now,' Aubrey said, his face creased with worry. 'I need all I have to stop the glacier melting. If I don't stop it, the thawed water will rush into the valley and wash away that village.'

Eve knew that Aubrey was right. But they needed to think fast to find a way to get the fairies to safety.

'What if Ingvar lowers her tail into the crevasse and the fairies grab hold of it, like a rope?' Eve suggested.

'Yes!' agreed Oscar. Eve picked her way along the edge of the crevasse to where the ice was flatter so that Ingvar could land. Oscar climbed down, carefully planting his feet next to Eve.

'Ing, can you reverse down into the crevasse?' Oscar asked, patting the dragon's back. 'Eve and I will hold onto you from up here. Your tail should just be able to reach the fairies.'

Ingvar was game for anything if it meant helping Oscar and Eve. She snorted and scrabbled at the ice with her front talons, then turned her body around and shuffled backwards into the crevasse, holding onto the ice with her claws. Eve and Oscar took hold of her front legs.

'Can you reach Ingvar's tail?' Oscar called down to the fairies.

From where Eve kneeled, holding onto

Ingvar, she could just make out the fairies reaching for Ingvar's pointed tail.

'It's too high – we can't reach it,' called Lilith.

'We can't risk letting Ingvar go down any further,' said Oscar. 'She'll fall, and it's too narrow for her to fly out.'

Eve frantically tried to think of a solution. There was only one thing she could do.

'Okay Oscar,' she said firmly. 'Hold on to Ingvar. I'm going down.'

Before Oscar could talk her out of it, Eve shimmied down Ingvar's scaly back, sliding legs-first until she was holding onto the dragon's tail like a rope swing. She stretched out her arm as far as she could reach, her fingers suspended in the cold air.

'Can you reach my hand?' Eve called to the fairies through gritted teeth, as she wrapped her legs around Ingvar's narrow tail and clung on with one arm. It was very dark inside the narrow crevasse and darker still when Eve looked down into the depths below. The creaking and cracking sounds were amplified down here. It was eerie.

'I still can't reach you.' Azura's voice sounded small and sad.

'I'm going to lower myself down so that I'm hanging from Ingvar's tail. You'll have to climb up me and up Ingvar's tail onto her back.' As she spoke, Eve realised just how cold it was inside the crevasse. She began to lower herself deeper into the depths. Her hands were already numb from the cold and the going was slow and clumsy.

'I can't hold on much longer!' Oscar called from above. His voice sounded muffled and far away.

Soon Eve was hanging down into the darkness, suspended, as both her hands gripped the forked end of Ingvar's tail.

'Grab my foot and climb!' she grunted to the fairies, straining to hold on.

Eve felt the weight of Lilith as her dainty fingers pawed their way up her body. For a horrible moment Eve felt her grip loosen as she took their weight, but she gritted her teeth and held on. Soon the fairy was climbing past her torso and over her head.

'Hurry!' called Oscar.

'Come on, Azura,' Eve urged. She felt the fairy begin to climb and soon they were eye to eye. The fairy's beautiful face was pale, and her lips were tinged blue. Her teeth chattered.

Just then the ice cracked again, and a large chunk broke away from the other side of the crevasse. It bounced down into the darkness, crashing onto the ice platform the fairies had been standing on only moments before. Azura closed her eyes in fear and gripped Eve tightly.

'Go, Azura,' Eve urged again. 'Climb.'

'I can't move!' Azura's voice was muffled as she buried her face into Eve's chest. She began to sob.

'Eve! Lilith is safe!' called Oscar. 'Eve! Where are you?' But his voice sounded like it was a world away.

$\mathcal{E}$ve and Azura hung suspended in the air, two bodies entwined, dangling in their icy prison. They were so close but Eve didn't have the energy to pull them both out. But she owed it to Ingvar and everyone who believed in her to try.

I'm coming Ing, she said to the dragon. *I'm coming.*

Eve closed her eyes and summoned all

of her strength. She focused on the power of the crystals. Her numb fingers suddenly felt hot as a fire radiated through her body. She could do this. Eve raised a hand, and gripped Ingvar's tail and began to pull herself upwards.

Little by little, drawing on everything she had, Eve hauled herself and Azura up Ingvar's tail and onto her back. Eve then passed Azura above her and Oscar was able to grab the fairy's hand and pull her to safety.

Eve crawled up Ingvar's neck and held out her hand as she reached the surface. Her arm felt almost too heavy to lift. Oscar's firm grip wrapped around her hand and she felt herself being lifted into the air.

She was safe but there was no time to lose. It took the strength of three fairies plus Oscar and Eve to pull Ingvar up. She looked hugely relieved to have four legs on the ice.

'I've stabilised the glacier,' said Aubrey, 'but I'll feel a lot better once we're out of here.'

'I'll say!' Eve agreed. As beautiful as this icy wonder was, Eve felt cold to her bones. She and Oscar clambered onto Ingvar's back while Aubrey tucked Lilith and Azura under an arm each. Aubrey took off, and Ingvar launched herself into the air and followed the fairies.

Eve felt the air temperature rise as they left the cold of the glacier behind. The sun felt warm on her skin, and she wrapped her arms around Ingvar and closed her eyes.

Long after they had left the bridge behind them, Eve, Oscar and Ingvar could still hear the sound of Percy the troll happily munching on his treasured corn chips.

'A haircut and a packet of corn chips. Who knew a troll would be so easy to please?' Oscar grinned.

Aubrey had flown ahead so that by the time they arrived in the fairy glen Lilith and Azura had been reunited with Orla. Eve could immediately see a change in the fairies. Their brush with death had given them cause to rethink their rebellion. By the remorseful looks on their faces it was clear they understood the terrible damage they could have caused.

'Good to see you,' Eve said to Orla as the Golden Queen gave her a warm hug.

'Thank you,' Orla whispered into her ear.

Azura looked at the ground, shy and uncertain. It softened her features. 'We're sorry.' She met Eve's gaze as she spoke. 'You saved our lives and we will never forget it.'

'I'm just glad nobody got hurt,' Eve replied,

and took both fairies by the hand.

'We realise we got a little carried away,' said Lilith, her cheeks flushed red. 'We've reached an agreement with Queen Orla.'

'What's that?' Eve asked. She felt a sense of relief that all seemed at peace in the fairy world now.

Lilith smiled, that same familiar cheeky smile. 'We'll do our work but every now and then we're allowed to play a prank on a human who has lost their sense of wonder at the natural world, or who is doing it harm.'

'I like it,' Eve laughed. 'A gentle reminder from the fairy world.'

Eve, Oscar and Ingvar feasted on a meal of fresh fruit and fairy delicacies before falling into a very deep sleep. Eve was dimly aware of pixie dust being sprinkled over their bodies as she drifted off.

Later, when they woke, Eve realised what

had happened. The fairies had worked their magic. Eve woke up in her own bed in Sylvie's house with Ingvar asleep in a ball on the end of her bed. Oscar snored gently from the mattress on the floor. Eve's gaze swept to the pink fairy door by her bed. The door was closed.

She lay back in her bed and closed her eyes. It felt good to be her normal size again. And as much as she loved their adventures, it always felt good to be home.

About the Author

Jess Black enjoys writing stories with heaps of action and humour. She has previously co-written *The Bindi Wildlife Adventure Series*, a fictional series about helping endangered animals around the world.

Now available in the series

KEEPER OF THE CRYSTALS
Eve and the Runaway Unicorn
JESS BLACK

KEEPER OF THE CRYSTALS
Eve and the Fiery Phoenix
JESS BLACK

KEEPER OF THE CRYSTALS
Eve and the Mermaid's Tears
JESS BLACK

KEEPER OF THE CRYSTALS
Eve and the Lost Dragon
JESS BLACK

KEEPER OF THE CRYSTALS
Eve and the Griffin's Gold
JESS BLACK

KEEPER OF THE CRYSTALS
Eve and the Hidden Giant
JESS BLACK

KEEPER OF THE CRYSTALS
Eve and the Rebel Fairies
JESS BLACK

For more riddles and
adventures visit
www.keeperofthecrystals.com.au